THE SECRET Sister

AYLA HASHWAY

DEDICATION

To my friends in Mrs. Dickerson's third grade class.

TABLE OF CONTENTS

Romy,

I hope you enjoy reading about Olivia's adventure!

– Ayla Hashway

ACKNOWLEDGMENTS

I would like to thank my mom for all of her help with this book. She inspired me to write a book of my own and kept pushing me to get over my writer's block that I had many times.

I would also like to thank my third grade class. They helped me get some of the characters' personalities.

- Ayla Hashway

CHAPTER ONE

THE BIG ANNOUNCEMENT

There once lived a girl named Olivia and her younger brother, Max. Olivia liked being older, mostly because she got to pick where she and her family went on vacation each year. Max didn't like being younger. He wanted to pick where to go on vacation. The only thing was, until Olivia was eighteen and went away to college, she would get to pick.

Beep, beep, beep went Olivia's alarm clock.

"Morning already?" Olivia asked as she threw a pink lacy pillow at her brother, Max, in his bed on the other side of the room they shared.

"Hey, what was that for?" Max asked.

"It's morning. Now go brush your teeth. I can smell your bad breath from here!" Olivia exclaimed, sitting up and fanning her nose.

"Oh yeah? Well, your hair is a mess!" yelled Max.

"You don't think yours is too?" Olivia asked.

"Olivia! Max! I have good news," called their mom from downstairs.

They scrambled out of bed and raced to the door. Olivia pushed Max into the door and made Max bump his head. As they rushed down the stairs, pushing one another back, Max tripped Olivia on the last step. He pulled the carpet tread covering the stairs right when she put her foot down and...*splat*!

"Ugh, thanks a lot, little bro," Olivia said angrily.

"Any time!" Max said with a smirk. "That

is how you get payback!"

"Very funny," Olivia said back, resisting the urge to strangle him.

Olivia got up and looked at the bruise on her kneecap that was turning a dark purple.

"What happened in there?" Mom called in a worried and concerned voice. "I heard a big crash."

"Max..." Olivia paused and thought should she really tell on her brother? He might hate her even more after that, and there morning had already gotten off on the wrong foot.

"Max what?" asked their mom.

"Max helped me up when I fell off the stairs." Olivia and her mother looked each other in the eye as Olivia and Max walked into the kitchen. "Now what's the big news?"

"Yeah, are we going to a zoo?" asked Max, jumping up and down.

“No, we are going on a vacation!” Mom told them.

“Yes!” screamed Olivia.

CHAPTER TWO

ABURA

Later that day, after Max broke his sneakers trying to put them on the neighbors' Great Dane, Mom, Olivia, and Max went to the mall.

"Olivia, Max and I are going to the shoe store. Where are you going, honey?" Mom asked as they walked into the mall.

"I guess I'll go to Hadley's across from the food court for some jewelry." Hadley's was Olivia's favorite store because they sold the cutest tote bags and other accessories.

"Okay. Be careful, and if you need anything, give me a call."

Olivia patted the cell phone in her pocket. "I will."

As Olivia was walking, she passed the bookstore and saw the two books she'd been wanting called *Blues Bones* and *Visions of Mockingbird Point*. Olivia went into the bookstore and straight to the display table in front. She picked up the books and debated if she should buy them both.

"Excuse me," one of the workers said. "Just so you know, both of those books are on sale for only $5.99 each."

Olivia's eyes lit up. "Wow! Thanks. I'll get both." She brought them to the counter and paid.

"Would you like a bag?" asked the man at the register.

"No. I'm fine," Olivia said, walking off and looking at the books in her hands.

Outside the store, a woman with brown hair, who was wearing short sleeves, shorts, and a half-broken star necklace that had “Sisters” written on it came up along side her. She smiled at Olivia and handed her a flyer.

“Have you ever been to Abura?” the woman asked her.

Olivia took the flyer and looked at the beach and boardwalk displayed on the front. “No, but I’ve been wanting to go there.”

“Oh, you would love this one waterfall,” the lady said. “At night it looks purple from the sunset reflecting on it.”

“Really? That’s awesome! Thank you for the flyer. I think I know where I’m going on vacation this summer,” Olivia said with a big smile. She put the flyer in her back pocket with her phone.

Olivia went to Hadley’s and saw a beautiful handbag that would be perfect for Abura. Then, she saw a golden feather necklace and a silver bracelet with her birthstone in the center surrounded by cubic zirconium. When she picked it up, it started shining and sparkling in the light. She liked the amethyst especially because it was purple, her favorite color.

She went up to the counter and paid for all three items. As she left the store, she counted the rest of her money. She only had ten dollars left.

On her way back to the shoe store, she noticed the woman who had given her the flyer on Abura was gone.

CHAPTER THREE

ANOTHER ARGUMENT

On the ride home, Olivia showed Mom and Max what she bought.

"Nice, honey," Mom said.

Max stuck his new sneaker in Olivia's face. "Look at my new shoes! They have skulls on the bottom!"

"Get this out of my face!" Olivia said, pushing his foot away. Although she didn't like having the sneaker in her face, she did think it was pretty cool with all the red highlights. Not that she would tell Max that.

"Oh," Olivia said. "I picked where we are going on vacation."

"Wait!" Max waved his hands in the air. "Can we go to Cape May or New York to go to the zoo?"

"No, we are going to Abura," Olivia said.

"What's Abura?" Max asked.

"It's a private island that I've wanted to go to since I was three or four." Olivia took the flyer out of her pocket and handed it to Max.

"Boring," Max mumbled, tossing the flyer on the floor.

"Excuse me!" Olivia shouted as she scooped the flyer back up.

"What? If you really wanted to go, you should have picked it the last eleven times. Plus, you don't even know when you started wanting to go. You're just making that up." Max pouted and crossed his arms.

Olivia leaned toward Max and whispered, "I'm not going to start another fight because of what happened last time when you tripped me."

"What so special about Abura anyway?" Max asked, rolling his eyes.

"There's this one waterfall that the sunset reflects on and makes it look purple."

"Sounds...cool?" Max said, obviously not impressed.

"You'll see how awesome it is when we get there."

"So it's in front of the airport?"

"I didn't mean literally when we get there." She kicked Max's leg. "Brothers," Olivia mumbled to herself so he couldn't hear.

Max tried to kick Olivia back, but she pulled her leg away just in time.

"Dang it!" Max said, slapping his leg.

"Ha-ha! Too bad, so sad."

Olivia looked at the brochure next to her. She couldn't wait to get there and see the gorgeous waterfall. Maybe it was even better than how it looked in the picture.

CHAPTER FOUR

BREAKING IN

As Olivia and Max ate their lunch, their mom was in her home office, talking on the phone and typing on the computer. All of a sudden, Mom got up and slammed the office door shut. Olivia and Max looked at each other.

Max shrugged and walked into the den.

"What do you...?" Olivia began to call after him, but she stopped when Mom started screaming and yelling. Her mom was talking so fast Olivia couldn't keep up and make out the words she was saying.

Then there was a minute of silence. Olivia knew something was wrong, and she was going to find out what. After a few more minutes passed, her mom came out of the office. Her face was all red from anger.

"Olivia, I'm going to be out for a little while."

"Where are you going? Is everything okay?" Olivia asked.

"I...I'm going to the food store. You're in charge until I get back." Mom grabbed her purse and went out the door.

Olivia waited two minutes to be sure Mom was gone. Then she went into the den and got Max.

"We need to sneak into Mom's office and check her computer to see what she was doing," Olivia said.

"Is Mom home?" asked Max, not even looking up from his iPad.

"No, she just left two minutes ago."

"Do you even know what Mom's computer

password is anyway?" Max asked. "Aw, come on!" he yelled at the game he was playing. He put it on the coffee table.

"Yeah, it's Sage26. She changed it last week when we got Sage." Sage was Olivia's brand new German shepherd puppy she got on the last day of school. "Come on now. We don't want Mom or Dad to see us in the office."

Olivia and Max tiptoed down the hall into the office. Olivia sat down and typed S-A-G-E-2-6 in all caps.

The page opened up to an e-mail with a strange link. Olivia spun in the desk chair, debating if she should read the e-mail or click on the link. She knew both would be bad because she would be invading someone's personal business, and that *someone* wasn't her.

"What are you doing?" Max asked. "Read it. Who is it from?"

"No, Max. I'm worried. What if it's something bad?" Olivia responded.

"Who cares?" Max said, squeezing onto the chair next to Olivia and spinning around to read the e-mail.

Olivia covered her eyes with her hands. "Who is it from?" she asked.

"Her sister," Max said.

"What?" Olivia uncovered her eyes and looked at the screen, but Max was leaning forward and his big head was blocking her view. "That's impossible. Mom doesn't have a sister."

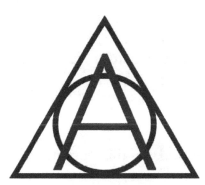

CHAPTER FIVE

THE E-MAIL

Olivia pushed Max aside. “Let me see the thing. Yesterday you thought a candy wrapper was a five dollar bill.”

Max pointed to the screen. “I told you it said sister!”

Olivia was so shocked she couldn’t look at anything but the word “sister” on the screen. “Why wouldn’t Mom tell us though?” she asked.

“I don’t know. Do I look like Mom?” Max asked.

“Yeah, kind of,” Olivia said with a smirk.

“Stop!” Max said, clicking on the Photo Booth icon on the bottom of the screen so he could check his reflection. “Come on!” he yelled.

“What?” Olivia asked. “You do look like Mom?”

“Yes,” Max grumbled.

Olivia closed Photo Booth and read the email.

Sara,

Have you told your family about me yet? If not, meet me at Pigeon Avenue on the corner of Route 305 and Secret Lane.

Your sister,

Amanda

“I’ve never in my life heard of Pigeon Avenue or Route 305 or Secret Lane,” Olivia said. “But that must be where Mom is going right now.”

"How are we ever going to get to Mom now?" Max asked.

"We could use the navigation system on my phone and ride our bikes," suggested Olivia.

"Okay, we just need to look it up now," Max said.

Olivia took her phone from her back pocket. "I am, but there is no sign of it. But Mom has a tracker on my phone. I can reverse it and track her!"

"For once I'm glad you're such a nerd."

"You're just jealous because I'm smarter than you and I have the trophies to prove it." Olivia had won several trophies for her inventions. One time she even had her invention featured in the newspaper.

A couple minutes later, Olivia had finished reversing the tracker. "Mom is in New Jersey still. Come on. Get your bike and let's go!"

Olivia shouted.

CHAPTER SIX

THE SECRET SISTER

They pedaled as fast as they could, following the tracker on Olivia's phone. After a while, they found their mom's car on the side of the road next to a building that looked more like a wooden hut than anything else. There was no parking lot or driveway. Only grass, mud, and gravel.

"Look, Max. There are Mom's footprints. We can follow them into the building," Olivia said, leaning her bike behind a big green dumpster on the side of the building. "Just be quiet and careful. We can't let Mom or her sister see us."

"Wait. What do you think was on the link in

the email?" Max asked, putting his bike next to his sister's.

"Don't know. Don't care," Olivia whispered.

They crept to the front door, which was cracked open. As they looked inside, they saw a lady with blond hair, hot pink painted nails, and a floral sundress.

"That must be Aunt Amanda," Max whispered to Olivia.

"Don't call her aunt. We don't know anything about her," Olivia said.

Amanda looked over and saw the kids but did not tell their mother they were there. Their mother had her back to them and they couldn't hear what she was saying.

When their mother turned in their direction, Max and Olivia ran for the dumpster and jumped inside. Olivia peeked out and saw her mother get into her car and drive away.

"Ahhhh!" Max screamed like a little girl.

"What is it? A snake?" Olivia asked.

"No, worse. A m-m-m-mouse!" Max mumbled.

"Yeah, it's right behind you," Olivia said, pretending to be scared.

"No, it's not!" Max said, realizing he'd been tricked.

"Well, now there is," Olivia said with a laugh.

"Ahhh! There's a rat! Oh wait. That's just your face." Max burst into laughter.

Olivia waited a couple of seconds and then tackled him. As Max went down, his hand touched the mouse's tail.

"Ew! I thought you were just joking about the mouse!" Max shrieked and fell backward out of the dumpster.

“When did my brother turn into a baby?” Olivia asked.

“Hey!” Max said. “I’m—”

Before he could finish, Olivia interrupted. “Wait. We have to get home before Mom, and she’s on her way already!”

Max looked around. “There’s a path through the woods. Maybe it’s a shortcut. We have an opening like that in our backyard.”

“We’ll have to find out,” Olivia said.

As they were biking, Olivia thought about Amanda. She seemed familiar for some reason.

CHAPTER SEVEN

THE SECRET PASSAGEWAY

The pathway finally came to a big opening. They were shocked to see it led directly to their backyard.

"Max, what do you think is going on?" Olivia asked, stopping at the edge of their yard.

"I don't know. Do you think Mom knows though?"

"I would guess, but she drove. She didn't take the pathway. So maybe not."

"Look, Mom's car is pulling into the driveway," Max said. "We have to get inside."

"Come on. Hide your bike under the back deck." Olivia took off for the deck and stashed her bike.

They ran up the stairs and to the sliding glass door, trying not to be seen. They went upstairs and turned left into their room. Olivia quickly grabbed her phone and Max looked around for his iPad.

"I left it in the den!" he said.

"Uh, play with Sage," Olivia suggested.

Max whistled for the dog. Sage came running up the stairs and burrowed under Max. When Max stood up, there was a big wet mark on the back of his pants.

"Ew! What is this?" Max asked as he tried to wipe it off.

"Drool, maybe?" Olivia suggested.

They quickly got back to what they were doing when they heard the front door open.

"Olivia! Max! I'm home. Where are you guys?"

"Upstairs in our room," they called down.

Then they both rushed down the stairs. They went into the living room to greet their mom.

"Where are the groceries from the store?" Olivia asked, looking at her mother's empty hands. She wondered if her mother would lie and keep going with the food store story or if she'd tell the truth.

"They didn't have the good chips and were out of ice cream sandwiches," Mom said. "I even checked with the workers, and they were all out of both. They said they would have some by tomorrow though."

"I guess there's always next time," Max said.

Max and Olivia went into the den.

"Mom lied to us again?" Olivia asked.

"Victory is mine!" Max said, grabbing the iPad from the coffee table.

"You're worried about an iPad after all that's happened in the past few hours?"

"Who wouldn't be?" Max asked, already playing his game.

"Um, smart people, so obviously not you."

"Die, zombies! Die!" Max yelled at the screen.

"Seriously?" Olivia said.

"Don't you have an invention to work on?" Max asked.

"Max, I'm not worried about them right now. What I'm worried about is all the stuff that's been going on. And why we never knew about Aunt Amanda. What did she do that made Mom keep her from us for all these years? If Mom's not going to tell us, then we'll have to find out for ourselves."

CHAPTER EIGHT

AMANDA WHO?

Olivia woke up at 5:00 a.m. to research Amanda Brooks on her phone. She'd been trying for two weeks to find information on her mother's secret sister. Since Mom was trying so hard to keep Amanda a secret, Olivia knew she wouldn't get anywhere by asking who she was. Mom's maiden name was Brooks, so Olivia had been searching Amanda and Sara Brooks, hoping to find anything about them.

So far, she hadn't found much on Amanda other than her first name being mentioned in Olivia's grandmother's obituary from when she died thirteen years ago before Olivia was born.

"Why is there nothing on Amanda?"

"What are you doing up this early?" Max asked, rubbing his sleepy eyes.

"I'm in the middle of researching Amanda and Sara Brooks."

"Still? You've been at it for three weeks!"

"Correction, two weeks."

"Just go back to bed. I'm tired," Max groaned.

"I won't until I find at least one more thing." Olivia continued to scroll through her search screen.

"Then you're going to be up for a while," Max said, covering his ears with his pillow.

Olivia got out of bed and removed the pillow from Max's head. "Listen. We need to sneak back into Amanda's yard and see what she's up to.

"Okay, wake me up at eight." Max rolled over to face the wall.

Five minutes later, Olivia heard snoring. “Max,” she called from her bed.

“Is it eight o’clock already?”

“No. You’re just snoring really loud. I can’t concentrate,” Olivia said.

When Max went back to sleep, Olivia found a picture of her mother, but the picture had been torn in half like someone else had been standing next to her.

“Who would post this?” Olivia whispered. “Someone must have the other half of the photo.”

Olivia looked over at her brother sound asleep again. She got out of bed and changed both the clocks in the room so they read 8:00.

“Max,” she said, standing over his bed. “It’s eight o’clock.”

“Ah! The rat’s back!” Max yelled as his arms flailed in the air.

"Be quiet." Olivia covered Max's mouth with her hand. "Mom must be sleeping in today. I'll leave her a note saying we're going for a bike ride before breakfast."

Olivia hoped they would find a clue at Amanda's house so she could figure out what she and her mother were up to.

CHAPTER NINE

BACK TO AMANDA'S

Olivia and Max got dressed and rushed downstairs. Olivia wrote the note while Max got their bikes out from under the deck. They set off on the path behind their house.

"Do you think Amanda is up to something?" Max asked.

"I found a picture of Mom online and it was cut in half. Do you think Mom and Amanda each have half?"

"Don't know, but if Amanda does have half of the picture, hopefully we'll find it and can sneak it in our room," Max said.

Olivia thought maybe Max was getting smarter as life went on. The only thing was

Olivia didn't think Max could handle being told that.

"Look. There's the opening to her hut," Olivia said, peddling as hard and fast as she could.

Max and Olivia stashed their bikes behind the dumpster again and peeked through the window on the front door, but Amanda was gone. All the furniture was gone too.

"Where is she?" Olivia asked, looking around the room.

"I don't know. Do I look like Amanda?" Max asked as Olivia handed him a mirror from her bag.

"Come on!" Max yelled.

"What, you look like her too?" Olivia asked.

"Yes," Max grumbled. "Why do I look like so many girls in the family?" Max asked as he handed the mirror back to Olivia.

"Come on. Let's go inside to see if we can find anything," Olivia said. She reached for the doorknob, and surprisingly it was unlocked.

"Maybe she moved," Max suggested. "Hey, do you think Mom made her leave town so we wouldn't find out about her?"

"Maybe. Or Amanda could have just been in town visiting, but then why would she take the furniture when she left?" There were still too many questions.

Olivia and Max walked into the living room. In the middle of the floor was a piece of paper. Olivia bent down to pick it up. "What is this? It has some kind of symbol on it."

"What kind of symbol?" Max asked, trying to see the paper.

The symbol was a triangle with a circle inside. In the middle was the letter A.

"It almost reminds me of the Deathly Hallows from Harry Potter," Olivia said.

"The D-deathly Hallows?" Max asked, biting his fingernails. "Do you think Aunt Amanda is working for Voldemort?"

"Yeah, she's working for Voldemort," Olivia said sarcastically. "She and Mom are both Death Eaters."

"Really—? Oh, you're kidding," Max said.

Olivia rolled her eyes as she looked up the symbol on her phone. "It says here that the symbol stands for an invention company called Original Artistry run by Amanda Walters."

"What? I thought Amanda's last name was Brooks," Max said.

"So did I, but that explains why when I tried to look her up, Mom was the only one who showed up," Olivia said.

"But then how are they sisters?" Max

asked.

“Easy, they must be half sisters!” Olivia exclaimed. “I read Grandma’s obituary online, and I found out she was originally married to someone named Alex Walters.”

“Look him up on your phone,” Max suggested.

Olivia looked up Alex Walters. While she was looking, she found a picture of Alex and her grandmother together at what looked like a fancy restaurant called All-Star. “It says he owns the restaurant too. It’s only about five miles away.”

“How can we sneak out again without Mom noticing?” Max asked.

“I don’t know, but we’ll have to figure out some way. We need to talk to Mr. Walters.”

CHAPTER TEN

MR. WALTERS

After lunch, Olivia and Max went into their mom's room and asked if she needed help packing their things for Abura.

"As a matter of fact there is something you can do for me. I need you guys to go to the store and get four luggage tags for our suitcases," their mom said. "Olivia, you're in charge."

As they walked out of the bedroom, Max said, "Why do you always get to be in charge. I'm ten, only two years younger. What's the difference?"

"The difference is I'm more responsible than you. If you really want to be in charge, then we'll race downstairs and see who wins. The winner is in charge." Olivia turned and pointed her finger at Max. "Also, no pulling rugs or pushing."

"Ready, set, go!" Max said.

They both charged down the stairs like a herd of elephants. Olivia beat Max by one foot.

"Ha! Still in charge," Olivia cheered while doing her victory dance.

"I let you win," Max said, but Olivia could see he was disappointed. He was lying to her, just like Mom had lied to them.

They walked through the kitchen and yelled good-bye to their mom. Olivia already had the directions to All-Star displayed on her phone when they walked out the door. Olivia and Max grabbed their bikes and started up the road.

"Just keep in mind we still have to run to the store to get those luggage tags for Mom,"

Olivia said.

"Can I just ask why we are going to that restaurant? What is Mr. Walters going to help us with?"

"He might know something about Amanda or Mom that we don't know and help us find more clues about what's going on."

"Okay, fine. I just hope my feet don't get tired from pedaling that long."

"Quit whining, you big baby," Olivia said.

After that, Max didn't even dare to say another word to Olivia.

Finally, they stopped at a gigantic building with sparkling lights around the name of the restaurant written in all caps. There were trees on both sides of the door and a blue and red awning above the door.

"Can we eat?" Max asked as he sniffed the air.

"Didn't we just eat lunch? And plus, we aren't here for that anyway," Olivia said, laying her bike on the ground.

"So? I smell a delicious steak."

"Max, we literally ate steak yesterday for dinner."

As they walked in, a bell rang and the hostess greeted them.

"Do you know where Alex Walters is?" Olivia asked. "We need to talk to him about something."

"Is Mr. Walters expecting you?" the hostess asked.

"No, but we are his grandchildren," Olivia told the woman. Max opened his mouth to speak, but before he could ruin Olivia's story, she said, "I'm Olivia, and this is my brother, Max."

"Okay, why didn't you say so earlier?" the

hostess asked. “Come right this way!”

On the way to Mr. Walters’s office, they walked slowly down the hall to admire all the chandeliers, paintings, and the red velvet carpet beneath them.

When they reached his open office door, the hostess knocked and said, “Mr. Walters, you have visitors.” She took a step back and motioned for them to go in. Then she speed walked back to the hostess station.

“Who are you?” Mr. Walters asked, standing up to greet them.

“Um, our grandmother is Lucy Brooks,” Olivia said.

“Lucy?” he said with wide eyes.

“Yes, she is our grandmother. I’m Olivia and this is my little brother, Max. We just found out our mom has a sister named Amanda Walters. Is she your daughter?”

Mr. Walters looked down. "Amanda, yes. Those two sisters...let's just say they were friends when they were little."

"What happened?" Olivia asked.

"Amanda got into her teens and then—"

"What's this thing?" Max asked, holding up a glass swan from Mr. Walters's desk.

"Don't play with that!" Mr. Walters said.

"Max, get over here," Olivia said, stomping her foot and pointing to the spot next to her.

Max started walking over, still holding the swan. As he walked by, Mr. Walters snatched the swan out of Max's hands. "Hey!" Max yelled.

"Stop yelling, Max. People in the restaurant might hear you," Olivia said.

"Yes. I'd appreciate it if you would keep your voice down." He put the swan down on the glass table next to him.

"What happened to Amanda?" Olivia asked.

"She started stealing things. Robbing banks was most likely going to be next, but I was wrong. She went to an engineering club and started making inventions," Mr. Walters said. "Your mom was so disappointed in her sister and mad at her she wouldn't ever talk to her no matter what, so no one even talks about Amanda being in the family. A little while later, Amanda was smart enough to open her own company called Original Artistry."

"What did she steal?" Max said, swinging from a chandelier.

"Get down from there, young man!" Mr. Walters yelled, pointing his finger at Max.

Mr. Walters walked over to get Max down from the chandelier. "What Amanda stole is none of my business or yours."

"Thank you, Mr. Walters," Olivia said. "Max, come on. Let's go." Olivia pushed Max through the door.

"Why are we leaving already?" Max asked.

"We're leaving because we're obviously not going to get any information out of Mr. Walters. He must be trying to protect Amanda."

"Well, what are we going to do now?" Max asked.

"I don't know, but we'll have to figure it out one way or another," Olivia said. She didn't know how though, since they were leaving for Abura the very next day.

CHAPTER ELEVEN

TO THE AIRPORT

Cuckoo cuckoo!

"Ahhhhh!" Olivia screamed at the sound of the cuckoo clock above the couch she was sleeping on at her grandmother's house over night.

Crash, bang!

Olivia fell face-first off the couch, onto the floor, and rolled on top of Max who was sound asleep.

"Come on! I wanted to sleep in!" Max yelled at Olivia.

Their mom came rushing in the room. "Who wants to go to...Abura?" she said noticing what had happened.

"Me?" Olivia said with a shrug and a slightly worried look.

Their mom looked at Olivia and then Max with a stern look on her face.

"She did it!" Max yelled before Olivia could say anything.

"The clock scared me. Plus Max was going to sleep in, and when he says sleep in, he means one more hour!" Olivia blurted out, getting Max back under the bus.

"Max, it might be 3:30 in the morning, but if you sleep in, you will miss the taxi and not be dressed or ready at all. You will even miss out on Abura! Now get dressed, and I will meet you in the living room," she said just so Max would not sleep in.

"But Dad is sleeping in!" Max complained.

"How can you tell?" Mom asked, looking around.

"I don't know. Maybe because I can still hear him snoring!" Max said, talking back.

"That's only because your grandfather kept talking and telling your dad about Abura all night. Well, at least it felt like it was all night," Mom said with a sigh.

"Tell me about it. I barely slept!" Olivia said, stepping into the fight.

"He is your father!" Max argued again.

"Max, stop it. We've been waiting over three hundred days to go on vacation. Let's not ruin it already!" she said in an annoyed voice.

Olivia quickly got up, grabbed her clothes, and went into the room across the hall to change.

"Dad?" she said startled. "I thought you were brushing your teeth by now!"

"No, I never left this room. By the way, keep it down. I don't want your mom to know

I'm in here sleeping in," their Dad said.

"Okay, first of all Mom knows you are sleeping in, and second of all I need to get changed. You are holding everyone up here!" Olivia said, handing him his toothbrush.

He finally got out of bed, took the toothbrush from Olivia, and went into the bathroom.

Olivia slammed the door shut behind him and sighed.

When she came out, she went back into the playroom and found Max sound asleep again. She went over and picked up the messy pile of clothes he was going to wear and threw them directly on his head.

"What the...?" Max said, surprised to find his clothes on his head.

"Go get dressed. The taxi is almost here!" Olivia called, starting to walk into the bathroom to brush her teeth so she could meet up with the others in the living room.

When Max was ready three minutes later, the taxi was there. Olivia stayed and waited for her grandmother to grab her carry-on upstairs in her room.

Olivia started to hear footsteps coming down the stairs. When her grandma was ready and downstairs, they went out the door together and caught up to the others.

“Come on. Hurry up!” called Max.

As Olivia stepped into the black van, Max pulled her into the seat next to him.

“Grandma, do you want to sit with us?” Olivia asked politely.

“I would love to dear,” said their grandma.

Olivia’s grandfather and father sat next to each other while her mom sat alone.

Their grandfather talked to the driver about

Abura the whole hour it took to get to the airport.

Olivia felt like she had heard the stories all one hundred times by then.

CHAPTER TWELVE

AN EXCITING RIDE

"Group three may now board the plane," said the voice over the loud speaker in the airport.

Olivia and Max waved to their grandparents since they were group five.

Their grandma blew them a kiss. "See you in a few minutes!" she said joyfully.

Their grandparents had been wanting them to go to Abura for a while so it was a big deal for them, Olivia, and her family.

As they boarded, they realized that someone was in Max's seat.

"Um, excuse me. My son is supposed to sit there with my father," said their mom, gesturing to Max.

"Sorry, but this is our seat. You see my husband booked it for the four of us, so I think you are wrong here," the lady said.

Olivia's mother took out the boarding pass for Max and showed the lady that the seat was his.

"Oh honey, can you recheck what seat we are in?" the nice lady said to her husband.

"Oh, it's the one in front of this row. Sorry," the husband apologized.

"Thank you!" Mrs. Lockhart said.

Once they sat down, Olivia peeked her head out from behind the seat and saw her grandparents coming. She waved, hoping one of them would see her.

Her grandfather saw her and waved back.

Olivia smiled and patted the seat next to her for her grandma to sit down.

When they were all seated, they looked at each other with smiles that went from cheek to cheek. Olivia felt like she was going to burst with excitement and joy!

Then the plane started on the runway and took off in flight.

Olivia and Max took out their gummy bears and started to chew as fast as they could so their ears didn't react to the plane starting and taking off.

Olivia saw the woman and her baby sitting next to someone and was disturbed by how the mother had to ask the guy to get up so she could change the baby's diaper.

"Whoa," Max complained while fanning his nose, which told Olivia that he wished he hadn't sat there and he wanted to be with dad on the other side in front of Olivia.

Olivia giggled, and then an announcement

came on over the loud speaker.

"We are coming close to a storm. We will have to taxi for a while," the voice said.

Then Olivia got an idea. She should invent a plane that was strong enough to go through storms so they would not have to taxi around in the air and be delayed like this. Then she realized that she didn't have her invention bag with her. It was in a different suitcase of hers.

"Here. You look tired," her mom said, handing her a neck pillow.

Olivia took it and fell asleep.

CHAPTER THIRTEEN

WELCOME TO ABURA

As Olivia stepped out of the airport, she saw how amazing Abura was. The beautiful green and brown palm trees swayed in the warm breeze.

"Max, look," Olivia said. "It looks like the picture on the brochure that the nice lady handed me at the mall."

"Olivia, no matter what you say, I still think that flyer is boring," Max said with out hesitating.

All of a sudden, their dad pointed to a woman who had red, curly hair, big sunglasses, and a floppy hat, holding a sign that read "Lockhart." "Sara, did you schedule for a taxi to pick us up?" Dad asked.

Mom shook her head. "No. Maybe the hotel did it for us."

As they all walked over to the woman, Olivia felt like she recognized her from somewhere. She was wearing a necklace, but whatever charm was at the end was covered by her sundress.

"Hi. Are you the Lockharts?" the woman said in a kind voice.

"Yes," Olivia's mother said.

"Step right in," the woman said as she opened the door of the taxi for them.

Olivia stared at the woman.

"What's with the look?" Max asked.

"I just feel weird about that woman," Olivia whispered as they got into the taxi.

"Why though?"

"Max!" Olivia said in a loud whisper.

"Keep it down. She's right there." She tilted her head at the woman in the driver's seat.

Olivia stared out the window as they drove to the hotel. Suddenly, she saw the sand and the sun reflecting on the turquoise water. "Wow!" Olivia said, dragging out the word.

"We're here," the lady said, pulling up to the hotel.

As they got out of the taxi, they saw palm trees by the doorway to the main lobby. The building was tall, and it looked like every room had a balcony. It had a red roof and was next to another hotel. The one they were staying in was the smaller of the two. It seemed like a very short walk to the beach. Olivia stood there in amazement, staring at the tall building. They were staying in the top floor penthouse.

"Well, we better go check in at the other building," Grandma said. "See you at dinner.

Remember we are meeting at Scala's."

Max shoved Olivia out of the way, pushed open the doors, and ran inside.

"Max, wait up!" Olivia said, chasing after him.

"Kids, am I right?" Olivia's father said.

"I don't know. I kind of wish I could go back to being a kid," Olivia's mother said, running to catch up with Olivia and Max.

Mr. and Mrs. Lockhart went to check in while Olivia and Max waited in the lobby. Olivia sat on a red chair while Max looked at the brochure stand next to his seat. He picked up a brochure on a fishing trip. He walked over and tapped on his dad's shoulder to show him the brochure.

"Hold on, Max," Mr. Lockhart said. "We can do that later. We need the key for the room first."

Olivia got up and went over by her parents and Max. “Mom, what are we going to do while Max and Dad go fishing?”

“We could go shopping,” her mom said, taking the room key from the woman at the check-in counter.

“Okay. That sounds like a great idea,” Olivia said.

They walked into the elevator and pressed the button for the penthouse suite. When they got there, they saw a two-floor suite with plants on the sides of the doors, red velvet carpeting, black couches, and a glass table. A chandelier hung from the ceiling in the middle of the room.

“All right, Max,” their father said, “we’ll unpack and head on down to the dock to start fishing while your sister and your mom go shopping on the boardwalk.”

Olivia went to the room she was sharing with Max. Olivia opened her suitcase and found a piece of paper inside saying that her luggage was inspected by the airline. She looked all around in the suitcase, unfolding everything, but she couldn't find her invention bag with her notebook in it.

"Oh no!" Olivia said, starting to pace. "It can't be gone!"

"What can't be gone?" Max asked.

"My invention bag. It's not here!"

"I'm sure it's just in another suitcase," Max said. "Now stop pacing before you bump into a wall."

Olivia spread out her invention sheets she didn't lose and put them into separate drawers.

"Olivia, please don't tell me you're hogging up all those drawers with your dumb inventions," Max said.

“First of all, they aren’t dumb, and you have your own set of drawers.” Olivia pointed to the second dresser.

“Well, I want more room for my stuff.”

“How much stuff did you bring?”

“Why do you need to know?” Max said, stepping back.

“Because I’m your older sister, and we tell each other most things. Including our thoughts about Amanda,” Olivia whispered so Mom and Dad wouldn’t hear.

“How can you think about her when we’re in paradise?” Max asked.

“So you’re going to spend your time in paradise fishing?”

“Not the whole time,” Max said, stretching out the word “whole.”

Olivia didn’t care what Max said. She had to figure out what was going on with Amanda and why she was gone.

CHAPTER FOURTEEN

A MYSTERIOUS DISAPPEARANCE

On the boardwalk, Olivia's mom stopped to look at a bracelet through the glass window of a store. It was gold with a turquoise stone in the middle.

"No way. This looks just like the one I had when I was younger. It went missing one day and I never found it."

"Do you want to go in and check it out?" Olivia asked.

"Sure. Why not?"

Olivia saw a hot pretzel stand along the boardwalk. "Oh, can I get a soft pretzel from the stand over there?"

"Sure. Just don't take too long." Olivia's

mom handed her a five dollar bill. Olivia walked over to the stand while her mom went into the store.

A woman with short blond hair with blue and purple streaks came up to Olivia and handed her a card. “This is to a tour at the waterfall. It’s for children your age.”

“Does the waterfall look purple at night from the sunset’s reflection on it?” Olivia asked, hoping it was the same one from the flyer on Abura.

“Why, yes. I think you’ll really enjoy it. The tour will begin at seven. I hope you can make it.” The woman leaned closer and whispered, “Just don’t tell anybody about it.”

“But why?” Olivia asked.

“Because it’s only for ages eleven to thirteen.”

“Why can’t parents come?” Olivia asked.

"The waterfall protects an island secret that's only visible to children your age." The woman winked and started to walk away. "Trust me. You don't want to miss it," she called back over her shoulder.

Olivia put the card in the back pocket of her shorts with her phone. She didn't know how she would sneak out with her mom and dad there, but she would have to in order to discover the secret behind the waterfall.

After Olivia got her soft pretzel, she went into the store, looking for her mom. She checked the whole store but couldn't find her. So Olivia decided to check with the store manager. The manager had black hair and an eyebrow piercing.

"Have you seen a woman with a turquoise pocketbook, blond hair, and green eyes, wearing black and white flip-flops and a sundress?" Olivia asked the woman.

"No, I haven't seen her. Sorry," the woman said.

"But she was just looking at the bracelet in the window."

The woman shrugged her shoulders. "I was busy helping a customer. She must have left because we are the only ones in the store now."

"Thank you," Olivia said and ran through the door. She took her cell phone from her back pocket and dialed her mom's number. After the phone rang six times it went to voice mail. "Hi, Mom. It's Olivia. Where are you? You weren't in the store, so I'm going to try to find Grandma and Grandpa. Call me back as soon as possible."

Olivia hung up and headed to her grandparent's apartment, but no one was there. "Oh, they must be at lunch since they didn't eat anything on the plane," Olivia said to herself. She decided to go to the dock to see if the boat Max and Dad had rented was back yet.

Max and Dad were still out on the water, so Olivia went back to the hotel. In the lobby, she asked the person at the main desk if her mom had returned.

"No. I'm afraid not," the woman said.

"Can I have another room key?" Olivia asked.

"Sure thing. Hold on." The woman handed Olivia a key to the room.

Olivia headed upstairs. She sat on the couch, waiting for Max and her dad to get back. And all the time she wondered where her mother was.

CHAPTER FIFTEEN

TIME FOR DINNER?

Max and Dad got back to the hotel around 5:30. Olivia paced around the room in circles.

"What are you doing?" Dad asked. "And where's your mother?"

"She's missing. When I went to get a soft pretzel, I came back and searched the whole store Mom was in looking at a bracelet. I checked with the store manager, too. I even tried calling her."

"Did she answer?" Max asked.

Olivia threw her hands in the air. "Would I be pacing around the room if she answered?"

"So no?" Max asked.

"Of course not!"

"I'll try calling your mother," Dad said. "Calm down." He went into the bedroom.

Olivia waited and waited. After what felt like an hour, her dad came back into the room and said, "She didn't answer and your grandparents said they haven't seen her either. I'm going to call the police."

A couple minutes later, the main lobby called up to their room to tell them that the police were there.

"Olivia, you're in charge while I go talk to the police in the main lobby," Dad said.

"Again?" Max yelled.

"Max, we don't have time for this," Olivia said as Dad rushed out the door.

A half hour later, Olivia was still pacing around the room while Max was complaining over and over again "I'm hungry! I'm hungry!" while jumping on the bed.

"Would you stop that before I get a serious headache?" Olivia said.

Max kept jumping. "Should Dad really be gone this long?" he asked.

"No. He should be back by now. I better go check on him." Olivia pulled her phone out of her pocket to try calling Mom again. The card for the waterfall tour fell out onto the floor, but she was too busy dialing to notice.

Olivia got Mom's voice mail again, although this time she didn't bother to leave another message.

When she got down to the main lobby, her dad was gone too, and so were all the police officers. Olivia walked up to the woman at the front desk.

"Did you see what happened to my father? He was just down here with the police."

"He talked to them for a while, and then

they all left together," the woman said.

"Thank you," Olivia said, rushing back to the penthouse suite. "Max!" Olivia screamed as soon as she opened the door.

"What happened?" Max asked, searching the kitchen for food.

"Dad left with the police, and I don't know what happened."

"Oh no!" Max yelled.

"I know, right?"

"There's no food. Who's going to buy me dinner?"

"Max! Dad is gone too and you're worried about dinner?" Olivia exclaimed.

"You're right. Grandma and Grandpa will buy dinner for me."

"We aren't going out to eat at all, Max! Snap out of it," Olivia yelled.

"I'm thirsty! I'm thirsty! I'm thirsty!" Max

repeated over and over again.

"Okay, I'll go get some ice from down the hall," Olivia said, rubbing her temples.

But Olivia didn't mean it. Instead, she planned to go to the secret tour of the waterfall. She knew she couldn't bring Max because he was too young, and it was obvious no matter what she did she wouldn't be able to find her mom and dad and still be able to go to the waterfall tour. Dad was with the police so he'd be fine, and Max would be safe in the hotel. Knowing him, he'd call their grandparents and try to convince them to take him out for dinner.

Olivia walked down the hall and made a right to get to the elevator. When she got to the main lobby, she checked her pocket for her phone. It wasn't there. She looked for the card for the secret tour, but that wasn't there either. She knew she would have to find the waterfall herself since she couldn't go back to the room without Max suspecting something, especially since she wouldn't have any ice for his drink.

Olivia didn't know how she would find the waterfall now.

CHAPTER SIXTEEN

THE PURPLE WATERFALL

Olivia hid behind a fake plant to make sure no one in the lobby saw her sneak out since they knew her parents were gone. When the woman working at the front desk went back into the room behind the check-in station, Olivia snuck out of the hotel.

When she got outside, she headed for the boardwalk. She saw a man selling some things at a stand on the side of the boardwalk. He looked like he lived in Abura, so she decided to ask him for directions.

“Excuse me,” Olivia said. “Do you know where any waterfalls are around here?”

“Oh yes,” he said. “You’re going to go straight down the boardwalk. Once you pass the fishing shop, make a left and then go straight until you reach a three-way path at the edge of a forest. You’ll make a right and then head straight until you reach the waterfall.”

“That’s a lot to remember,” Olivia said.

“If you would like, I could write the directions down for you.”

“Yes, thank you. That would be nice.”

When the man was finished writing, he handed the sheet of paper to Olivia and she started on her way.

“Be warned,” the man said. “The forest is rumored to be haunted. People hear a lot of weird noises in those woods.”

“What kind of noises?” Olivia asked.

“I don’t know and I don’t want to find out.” He raised one eyebrow. “You aren’t going there alone, are you?"

"No, definitely not." Olivia couldn't mention the secret tour. She hurried along.

She was anxious to get to the waterfall. She couldn't wait to see what kind of stuff would happen on the tour. Would she get more ideas for inventions to make?

Although she was kind of worried about the rumor the man told her about, she was excited to find the waterfall. After all, it was a secret tour. But the woman who had given her the card seemed too nice to be trying to trick her.

As Olivia got closer and closer, she started to hear those noises the man had warned her about. She kind of wished the kids on the tour were allowed to bring their parents, but it wasn't like Olivia could have brought her mom or her dad.

Olivia began to think about her parents

more than the noises, and she got worried. Were the police and her dad able to find her mom? Was Dad missing too? And was Max okay? Was he really responsible enough to handle being on his own? Would he starve to death?

“Everything’s going to be okay. Max is probably with Grandma and Grandpa. Dad is fine with the police, and I bet they found Mom by now. They’re probably on their way back to the hotel,” Olivia said, trying to calm herself down.

When Olivia reached the three-way path, a family of iguanas was blocking the path she needed to take to get to the waterfall. It looked like some of them were sleeping. Olivia would have to go another way. She figured there must be another way to get to the waterfall, even if it was longer.

Suddenly, she saw a whole group of gnarly trees with an opening that was just big enough for her to squeeze through. She ducked into it and came out on the other side of the iguanas.

"Well, at least something isn't going wrong today," Olivia said, happy to be back on the right path.

Up ahead, she saw a purple glow through the trees on the path. "That must be the waterfall!" Olivia exclaimed, jumping up and down. She started to run.

As she got closer, she ran faster and faster. Finally, she was there. The wind blew her long blond hair to the side as she stood before the waterfall and stared at its... She couldn't think of a word to describe it. It was almost magical.

All of a sudden, Olivia saw footprints that led toward the waterfall. They looked like Max's footprints with the skull imprints. Olivia got worried.

“This is all my imagination. That is not Max’s footprint,” she told herself, but she couldn’t get rid of the feeling that Max could be in danger.

CHAPTER SEVENTEEN

THE SECRET OF THE WATERFALL

Before Olivia could inspect the footprints, someone who looked exactly like Aunt Amanda appeared from behind the waterfall.

"Olivia!" Aunt Amanda said, walking over to her with her arms held up in the air. "I'm so glad you showed up."

"Huh?" Olivia took a step back.

"Your mother hasn't told you about me? My name is Amanda, and I'm your aunt."

Why would Aunt Amanda be here? Olivia wondered, thinking back to when she and Max were at Amanda's house. Olivia decided she should be very careful around Amanda, knowing what she found out about her. The longer she was around Amanda, the more uncomfortable Olivia got. But she couldn't let Aunt Amanda know that she knew so much about her.

"You know, I've always wanted an aunt," Olivia said, pretending to be joyful and putting a smile on her face.

Aunt Amanda put her arm around Olivia's shoulders. "I think we're going to get along just fine," she said, stretching out the word "fine."

"I'm sure you're right," Olivia said, playing along.

"I hear you are an inventor. I am too. Maybe we can make some inventions together."

"Absolutely," Olivia said.

"Come on in. I'll show you my inventions."

"Come in where?" Olivia asked, looking around.

"I made my own laboratory behind the waterfall. There's a door hidden on the other side of it. Come on. I'll show you." Aunt Amanda gestured for Olivia to follow her.

Aunt Amanda led Olivia around the sparkling waterfall. In between the palm trees they went. They walked between the waterfall and the mountain. Aunt Amanda went over to a keypad on the side of the rock mountain.

Olivia was confused. "Where is the door?"

"Just wait and you'll see." She typed in the pass code, but Olivia couldn't see what it was. Then all of a sudden, the rocks moved like the door to an elevator. Inside was a seating area with a table and a desk.

"Wow! This is a-amazing," Olivia stammered. "Am I really inside a mountain?"

"You haven't even seen the best part—my invention room. Right this way and I'll show you."

Olivia followed Aunt Amanda into the back of the room. Aunt Amanda put her thumb up against a touchpad that was hidden behind a large potted palm tree, and another door slid open.

Aunt Amanda told Olivia to go in first. She took Olivia into a room filled with all her inventions. The tallest one stood in the middle all the way at the other end of the room. Olivia ran toward it.

"What is it?" Olivia asked, eager to know what it was.

"That? That's the one I'm working on. It's not even done yet. Do you want to help me with it?"

"Of course! Yes! I mean...that's cool," Olivia said, feeling like the cat got her tongue.

"Great! Let's get started," Aunt Amanda

said, gathering tools to work on the invention. "Where's your brother?"

Olivia was so caught up in all the inventions that she forgot she left Max in the hotel room so she could go on the tour of the waterfall. "Oh yeah, is there a tour around here by the way? I'm supposed to be at it."

"A tour? Oh yes, I was going to hold one, but no one showed up except you."

"But who was the woman who handed me the card for the tour? Does she work with you?"

"Something like that. She's just a friend." Aunt Amanda waved her hand in the air like it didn't matter.

"What is this invention?" Olivia asked, getting caught up in everything around her. She tried to snap herself out of thinking Amanda was actually a good person, but the invention in front of her was an office tower with a chair and desk in each little bubble. She had never seen anything as magnificent as it before.

"All offices in the United States of America will have this invention. It will save them lots of room and lots of time."

"Wow, that is amazing. Do you think I can have just one portion for when I work on my inventions?" Olivia asked kindly, still trying to play along with her cover.

Part of Olivia wasn't lying when she said she wanted one portion of the office tower for working on her inventions. Somewhere inside, Olivia felt like Aunt Amanda wasn't bad after all, like Mr. Walters had said before. Even if Aunt Amanda was evil, Olivia felt like she could still change over time, no matter what she had done in the past. She even started to think her mom should forgive Aunt Amanda for what she had done in their childhood.

“Olivia? Olivia?” Aunt Amanda called, waving her perfectly manicured hand in front of Olivia’s face to get her attention.

“Oh, sorry about that. I guess I got a little too amazed by all of your inventions,” Olivia said, shaking her head to get out of the trance she was in.

“Thank you!” Amanda said. “And sure, we can make one extra portion of the office tower for you to take home and work on inventions with.”

Amanda was finally winning over Olivia.

CHAPTER EIGHTEEN

A SHOCKING DISCOVERY

Olivia and Aunt Amanda were working on the invention. They had already accomplished four office bubbles stacked on top of each other and even the one for Olivia.

"Olivia, can you get me the pliers with the red handles over there on the right corner of my desk please?" Aunt Amanda asked Olivia nicely, pointing to the wooden desk across the room.

"Sure, I guess so," Olivia answered, starting to walk over toward the desk.

When Olivia got to the desk, she saw a silver necklace sparkling in the light of a lantern. The necklace was a star that was broken in half and had the word "Sisters" carved into it. Olivia took a step away from the necklace, and she had a flashback to when the nice lady at the mall handed her the flyer to Abura and how she mentioned the waterfall. All of a sudden, the flashback stopped.

Olivia gasped and then whispered to herself, "That lady at the mall was Aunt Amanda! She was luring me here this whole time? Does she have my parents and Max?"

Olivia quickly grabbed the pliers and rushed over to Aunt Amanda, hoping she didn't suspect anything suspicious.

"What took so long? Are you feeling all right?" Aunt Amanda asked with fake sweetness.

"I just got dizzy and my stomach is starting to hurt. Can I use your bathroom?" Olivia said, trying to buy herself time to look for her parents.

"Sure thing. Just go straight down the hall and make a right at the end of it," Aunt Amanda answered.

"Thank you," Olivia said, putting her hands over her stomach and rushing toward the hallway.

As Olivia was leaving the room, she saw Aunt Amanda shake her head and stick out her tongue in disgust. "Sounds like that toilet is going to need some serious cleaning," she said.

Olivia still knew that she couldn't take too long to find her parents before Aunt Amanda started to suspect something. And that wasn't going to be easy since Olivia didn't know her way around her aunt's laboratory.

CHAPTER NINETEEN

A CLOSE CALL

Olivia got to the end of the hall and saw a banner with Aunt Amanda's company logo on it. The logo was written in red, black, and green coloring. The banner began at the gray shag flooring and reached to what seemed like door height.

Then Olivia stretched out her arm and pulled the silky smooth banner out of the way. She couldn't believe her eyes.

"Wow," Olivia whispered to herself, her eyes widening in disbelief.

Behind the banner was a passageway. At least it seemed like a passageway, but the only thing was there was a pass code to get in.

"What is the pass code? It could be anything," Olivia said, tapping her foot on the carpet gently while biting her fingernail and trying not to make much noise.

All of a sudden, she heard footsteps coming her way. Olivia quickly put the banner back in place and headed across the hall for the bathroom. She gently closed the door, not even making a peep. Olivia ducked down and looked underneath the bathroom door through the little crack.

Aunt Amanda came to the end of the hallway and bent down to inspect something. Olivia realized it was her footprint dented in the plush carpet. Aunt Amanda scowled. Olivia covered her mouth and crawled back away from the door as Aunt Amanda came closer. Olivia started to feel scared. Then she heard a triple knock on the bathroom door.

"Olivia, is everything all right in there? If you want, I can call your mom," Aunt Amanda said calmly in a concerned voice, but Olivia could tell she was faking the whole thing and it was all a trick.

"No, I'm good. Thanks anyway. Plus, your friend said only people my age are allowed here," Olivia said, playing along in hope of finding her parents.

Olivia knew she was trapped, but no matter what, she had to find her family.

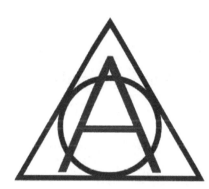

CHAPTER TWENTY

THE HIDDEN PASSWORD

Olivia went into the seating area and sat in the chair while Aunt Amanda worked on decorating the inventions in the other room.

Olivia sighed, wishing her family could be normal for once. Olivia started to spin on the chair with a bored look on her face. Then she began to neaten up Aunt Amanda's desk.

In one pile she saw a paper that looked like it was torn and a photo too. The photo was ripped down the middle and had her mom's image on it. Olivia remembered when she found the same picture online when she was back home with her parents and Max.

"It is all my fault," Olivia said as a tear ran

down the side of her cheek.

She looked back toward the hallway wishing she was with her family again.

Then she saw a sign above the doorway that said "2halves" on it.

Could that really be her password? Olivia thought.

"Aunt Amanda can I use the bathroom? I think I feel something coming on again," she said, pretending to not feel well.

"Sure, use it when you need to. You don't have to ask me," Aunt Amanda said sweetly.

"Thanks," Olivia said, rushing down the hall.

Olivia let out a sigh in relief that Aunt Amanda might have bought her excuse.

When Olivia got to the end of the hall she ran her hand down the banner gently, feeling proud she had come this far.

Olivia pulled the banner back and typed in "2halves" for the pass code to open the door. The door slid open to the left. Olivia quickly ran through the passageway before the door could close on her.

CHAPTER TWENTY-ONE

BEHIND THE DOOR

Olivia tried to walk forward, but she couldn't. She turned around and saw that her T-shirt was caught in the door. Olivia tried tugging, but it was useless. The shirt wouldn't budge. She saw tools hanging on the wall. All of a sudden, her eyes caught hold of the scissors.

Olivia paused for a second to think. Then she pulled forward to try to reach the scissors, but only her fingertips touched them. She tried again, and this time, she grabbed the scissors off of the rack. Olivia took the scissors and cut her shirt so she could get free. Olivia walked up the stairs and saw what looked like jail cells.

Olivia stopped and gasped. "Mom, Dad,

Max!"

"Olivia!" they all cried in unison.

Olivia quickly ran over and tried to free her mom, but it was no use. The cells were locked, and the bars were too strong for her to get her mom out.

"The lock. I just need to find the key to get you guys out!" Olivia said, looking around.

"Look over there behind the paper on the wall," Max said, pointing at the paper.

Olivia rushed over, lifted the paper, and saw a safe.

"How did you know something was there?" Olivia said, surprised that Max knew something for once.

"I saw her in there after she locked us up," Max said, still trying to get out on his own. "But I never got to see what the pass code was."

"It's a scanner though," Olivia said confused.

"Olivia, come here. I just might know what she would scan in for the pass code," their mom said.

Olivia rushed over to her mother, who was taking off her necklace. She handed it to Olivia through the bars of the cell.

Olivia looked at it closely and realized it was the other half to the necklace Aunt Amanda had, except it had the word "forever" carved into it.

Olivia rushed over to the safe and scanned the necklace.

She stepped back as the safe opened, and inside was the key.

CHAPTER TWENTY-TWO

THE CONFRONTATION

Olivia ran as fast as her legs could possibly go.

"Olivia!" Max said, holding his hand out in her way so she couldn't go any further.

Olivia stopped as soon as she could so she didn't run into his arm. "What, Max? I can't take all day, otherwise Aunt Amanda will suspect something," she said.

"Can you free me first please?" Max asked.

"What? Why should I free you first if you came here without me knowing and had no clue what you were doing?" Olivia said, obviously annoyed at Max.

"Well, the card fell out of your pocket,"

Max said.

"You should have given it back or told me!" Olivia said. "You know what? I don't have time for this!"

Olivia walked past Max's cell and over to her mom's. Without another word, she unlocked it.

Once she had freed everyone, they started heading down the stairs.

"Wait. We have to split up, so Max will go over there, and Mom over that way near me, and Dad behind Aunt Amanda," Olivia whispered to the others.

They all nodded in agreement before closing the door quietly behind them.

Then Olivia walked down the hall toward Aunt Amanda, who was working on an invention. Before Olivia said anything, she saw Aunt Amanda had a belt with a pouch on it and sticking out of it was Olivia's pink invention notebook.

Olivia's face turned red with anger when she saw behind her was her invention bag she had lost at the airport that very day.

"That's it!" Olivia screamed out loud.

Aunt Amanda turned around and saw Olivia filled with anger.

"What is wrong?" Aunt Amanda said kindly, pretending to be concerned.

"You know what's wrong! You took my invention bag, my notebook that was in it, stole my ideas, and worst of all you took my parents and Max, all because you wanted to lore me here to help you get more ideas!" Olivia yelled.

"Don't talk about it or your parents will get it, you little brat!" Aunt Amanda threatened.

"How are you going to do that when they are surrounding you?" Olivia said with a smirk.

"What?" Aunt Amanda said confused. "They are locked up!" Aunt Amanda chuckled, thinking Olivia was joking.

"Olivia freed us," their mother said, stepping out from behind the desk. "You don't have to do this. I see good inside you." She held up her half of the star necklace.

"Sara, that was the past. This is the present. We are free to do what we want. We aren't children like them anymore," Aunt Amanda said, gesturing to Olivia and Max. "Tell me if you change your mind about being evil and you want to join forces. We could rule this world together."

"I think I'll pass on that offer," Sara said, feeling good about herself.

"Very well then," Aunt Amanda said with a smirk while escaping down the other hall.

Olivia and the others ran after her.

At the other end of the hall, a door led to the outside. They reached it just in time to see Amanda disappear inside a helicopter.

As Olivia watched it fly away, she knew Aunt Amanda would be back for revenge and to steal Olivia's invention notebook once again.

ABOUT THE AUTHOR

Ayla Hashway is nine years old. She loves reading and writing. *The Secret Sister* is her first book, although she's been writing for years. She believes if you keep trying, you can make your dreams come true.